Darius Quinton Coleman, Boy Genius

PRAISE FOR *STORYSHARES*

"One of the brightest innovators and game-changers in the education industry."
– Forbes

"Your success in applying research-validated practices to promote literacy serves as a valuable model for other organizations seeking to create evidence-based literacy programs."

- Library of Congress

"We need powerful social and educational innovation, and Storyshares is breaking new ground. The organization addresses critical problems facing our students and teachers. I am excited about the strategies it brings to the collective work of making sure every student has an equal chance in life."
– Teach For America

"Around the world, this is one of the up-and-coming trailblazers changing the landscape of literacy and education."
- International Literacy Association

"It's the perfect idea. There's really nothing like this. I mean wow, this will be a wonderful experience for young people."   - Andrea Davis Pinkney, Executive Director, Scholastic

"Reading for meaning opens opportunities for a lifetime of learning. Providing emerging readers with engaging texts that are designed to offer both challenges and support for each individual will improve their lives for years to come. Storyshares is a wonderful start."
- David Rose, Co-founder of CAST & UDL

Darius Quinton Coleman, Boy Genius

Kelly Winters

STORYSHARES

Story Share, Inc.
New York. Boston. Philadelphia

Published in the United States by Story Share, Inc.

Storyshares
Story Share, Inc.
24 N. Bryn Mawr Avenue #340
Bryn Mawr, PA 19010-3304
www.storyshares.org

Inspiring reading with a new kind of book.

Interest Level: Middle School
Grade Level Equivalent: 3.1

9781642611434

Book design by Storyshares

Printed in the United States of America

Storyshares Presents

1

My mom figured out she had a problem on her hands when I was three.

She was taking a nap on the couch. I was supposed to be taking a nap in my room.

I found a screwdriver in the hall closet upstairs and took apart the safety gate at the top of our stairs. Then I went downstairs and dragged a stool across the kitchen floor, climbed up on it, and ate all the cookies she had hidden in the cupboard.

When I was four, I took apart the TV. When I was five, I put it back together.

When I was six, I was already making money by fixing fans, radios, and clocks for adults.

What I can't do, at least not very well, is read. I can look at a machine and then go home and draw every part of it, from memory. But don't ask me to read the instruction book about how to use it, because I won't remember a word of it. I'll figure that out by doing it.

My parents say I'm just like my great-grandfather, Darius Quinton, the first black aviator on Long Island. Back in 1916 he built his own airplane, and flew it. He also invented all kinds of crazy machines. He left behind a lab filled with his drawings, his machines, and his airplane.

I inherited all of it. I also inherited his name. I'm Darius Quinton Coleman. Some people call me the Boy Genius.

My mother also inherited his mechanical ability, and she's the one who passed it on to me. She's an artist who paints portraits for a living, but she can make or fix pretty much anything. She made a spinning wheel out of an old bicycle wheel, spun up a lot of yarn, and knitted me a sweater. She built a greenhouse in our yard, using old windows other people threw away. She built a beehive out of boards from a shed the neighbors tore down, and caught a swarm of wild bees to live in it. Every morning we have honey from that hive on toast.

My dad is a math professor at the New York Institute of Technology. He is not mechanically minded. He can change a light bulb, that's about it, but he's not exactly stupid, either.

We all live in my great-grandfather's house, a big, old, rambling place overlooking Clammer's Bay and Long Island Sound. He built it back in 1920 with money he made from his inventions.

When I was little, my great-grandfather was an old, old man, but still as smart as ever. He taught me his version of the principles of physics: "A body in motion, stays in motion until friction stops it. A body at rest, stays at rest. So, Darius, never rest. Keep moving, and keep learning."

He died when I was ten, and he was 110 years old. His gravestone says, "Friction Finally Got Me."

I still miss him. But I try to follow his advice, and I'm going to be an inventor like him.

2

One Saturday, I was sitting in my lab. I was drawing a machine that I wanted to invent. It was a wasp-killing machine. My mother would be happy, because the wasps were always trying to get into her beehive and kill the bees.

Someone knocked on the door. I looked out the window. It was a kid. At first, it looked like a boy. But when I opened the door, I saw that it was a girl. A girl who lived two houses down from mine.

"Hi, I'm Annie," she said. She was wearing running shoes, jeans, and a shirt that said Green Bay Packers. She had muscles in her arms like a boy, and a boy's way of walking. Her hair was braided into tight cornrows.

"Hi, I'm Darius," I said.

"I heard you're a genius," she said.

"Some people say that," I said. I don't like to brag.

"Listen, if you're so smart, maybe you can help me with something. I have a mystery."

I love a good mystery. I had never had the chance to solve one before, but I had always wanted to.

"OK, what's your mystery?" I asked.

"You know the empty house in between your house and my house? Some new people moved into it a couple of weeks ago. And they're odd. Not odd in a fun, interesting way, but odd in a way that might be criminal. In fact, I think they're crooks."

"What do you think they're doing?"

"That's the problem. I don't know. But they're very secretive. They don't talk to anyone. They always have all their shades down."

"They could just be shy."

"I don't think so. I saw them, and they look pretty tough. Not shy."

"Are they those three white guys who drive that black Cadillac?"

"That's them."

"I've seen them when I'm out on my bike." One blond, one brown-haired, and one with red hair. Otherwise they all looked alike. Tough. And mean.

"What do you think they're doing?" I asked.

"I have no idea. I just think they're up to something."

"Why don't you call the cops? Or tell your parents?"

"You know how adults are. They never believe anything a kid tells them. They'd say I was being overdramatic."

She was right. I had heard adults say that before. My parents usually didn't. They would probably be interested if I told them about these shady new neighbors. But I like to solve my own problems. It's more of a challenge that way.

"Sounds like you have a case," I said. I put out my hand for her to shake. "Delighted to work with you, Annie," I said. "Come on in."

3

I love to see the look on people's faces when they see my lab. It's an old barn with huge skylights in the roof. Filled with sunshine, but also filled with machines. All kinds of machines, from many years ago. Big brass gears, levers, pulleys, drive belts, drive chains, telescopes, distillers, generators, test tubes, dials, steam engines. And at the back of the barn, hanging from the rafters under the biggest skylight of all, my great-grandfather's hand-built airplane, the Spirit of Freedom.

When you open the door of the lab, it trips a lever. The lever makes brass gears spin. The gears set drive belts in motion. They start steel balls rolling. The balls hit other balls, which ride along tracks set into the walls. A rolling chain of motion, things falling, bells ringing, lights turning on, motors lifting up more steel balls, which spiral down curling tracks past musical metal prongs, bouncing into tunnels, hitting switches, turning on all the lights and the radio. It's amazing to watch and listen to, and it always makes me laugh. Just from opening the door, you get all kinds of energy and sound and movement. It's like my great-grandfather is saying, *Let your mind wake up. Let the thinking begin.*

Annie stood in the doorway, watching all the steel balls rolling, gears turning, lights turning on. She lifted her eyes to the high ceiling, looking at the bright blue plane with its wide white wings.

"Wow," was all she said.

She looked around at the tables full of tools, beakers, burners, test tubes, goggles, and heavy gloves. On the walls were old posters showing men and women in flying machines. Many of them featured my great-grandfather standing next to his plane.

"Where did you get all this stuff?" she asked.

"It was my great-grandfather's. He was an inventor."

"What did he invent?"

"He invented a very small, very necessary screw. Every motor on the planet has that screw in it. He only made one one-hundredth of a penny on each one he sold, but he sold a lot of them. Millions. Then he used the money he made to pay for his other inventions."

"What else did he invent?"

"He started out trying to make a flying machine. Have you ever seen those old movies of people trying to invent machines that would fly? Guys wearing goggles and riding contraptions with wings, trying to get off the ground? That was him."

"Cool."

"He didn't invent anything that could fly. But after the Wright brothers invented the airplane, he built one like theirs. He was the first black aviator on Long Island, back in 1912. He used to go to the Hempstead Plains and fly his airplane--they called them 'aeroplanes' back then."

"Wow. What else did he do?"

"He invented all kinds of things that you will never see. Tiny parts. But they're all needed to make other machines work. See those old wooden filing cabinets over there? They're full of drawings of all the ideas he had. I think he was way ahead of his time. I think someday, people will look at his drawings and think, 'Oh, that's what he was doing! Let's make this thing!' and it will turn out to be just what humanity needs."

"This is amazing," she said. She looked around some more. "It's like a museum."

"Except it's more fun than a museum because I get to use everything in it. Except the airplane. My parents won't let me fly it. Yet."

She sat down at my drawing table.

"OK," I said, "Tell me about these criminal neighbors."

4

She told me everything she knew, which was not much. They were three white guys who drove a big black car. They spent most of their time at home. They were not friendly. They kept all their shades down, all the time. She was right: that wasn't much evidence. Any adult who heard it would tell us to leave them alone and mind our own business.

"The first thing we have to do is watch them," I said. "We have to see what their pattern of movement is. When they go in, when they go out, and what they do."

"I tried that," she said. "But when they saw me looking at them from the woods between my house and theirs, they came outside and yelled at me to get lost."

"We have to watch them, but not let them see us doing it," I said. "Let's go see what the terrain looks like."

We went through the hilly woods between my house and the crooks' house. Big old trees and big old rocks. Some of the rocks in there were as big as cars. Annie's house was on the other side of their house.

"I have an idea," I said. "Come back to the lab. Let's build a periscope."

"A periscope? Isn't that something they use on submarines?"

"Yes. But you can use them on land, too, when you want to spy on someone. Are you any good at making things?"

She smiled. "Now you're talking. I can build anything. I love making stuff."

We went back to the lab. I drew a diagram of what we needed to do.

All we needed were some scrap boards, a couple of small mirrors, some sawing, gluing, and nailing, and we were all set. Annie was right: she was good at building things with wood. When I hammered, I bent every other nail. She could whack them in perfectly with just a few hits. We had our periscope. We painted it with splotches of black, green, gray, and brown. Camouflage.

Then we went back to the woods behind the crooks' house. We hid behind a big, car-sized rock and raised up the periscope, so we could look over the top of the rock. We could see the side and back of their house perfectly, but they couldn't see us. It was a big, fancy house. A mansion. Every window had the shades down. It looked like no one was home.

We took turns watching all afternoon.

Nothing happened.

No one went in. No one went out.

Late in the day, we smelled laundry. We could see steam coming out of the dryer vent on the side of their house. We could smell that nice, clean smell.

"What boring criminals," Annie said. "You never think of crooks doing laundry."

"I guess everyone has to," I said. "Even criminals. Let's quit for the day. Meet me tomorrow afternoon and we'll think of something else."

5

The next day was Sunday. My dad had to go to the hardware store to get some light bulbs. Like I said, my dad is not a mechanical genius, but he can change a light bulb. I went with him. I love hardware stores. They're filled with so much stuff, and they always give me ideas.

One of the crooks, the blond one, was in line in front of us at the checkout. He did not look like someone who spent his afternoons doing laundry. His clothes were dusty and he had B.O. But when he paid, I saw that he had a giant roll of $20 bills in his pocket. He was buying a bunch of laundry soap, bleach, and cleaning chemicals. I secretly thought he should buy some shampoo to go with his gallon-size jug of Formula 827, "Gets Out Grease Every Time!"

In addition to the light bulbs, my dad had bought fifteen packets of vegetable seeds, a pack of gum, some bird seed, a screwdriver, a and some dish soap.

The clerk said to my dad, "That will be $38.26."

My dad said, "Check it again. It should be $37.82."

Sure enough, he was right. One of the prices in the register was wrong. You can't fool my dad when it comes to numbers.

Annie showed up at the lab after my dad and I got home. We got the periscope and went to our spot behind the rock. This time we saw that same crook coming home from town. He must have gone to other places besides the hardware store. He had his bag from the hardware store, and two bags of groceries. He carried all that stuff inside. After a while we smelled the laundry smell again.

"This is so boring," Annie said. "All they ever do is wash their clothes."

"You'd never know it," I said. "I saw the guy. His clothes were filthy. And he stank."

"That's odd," she said.

"You're right. It is odd. What kind of criminal does a lot of laundry, but they're not washing their clothes?" I asked.

"Criminals always want money. Maybe they're money launderers," she said.

"What is money laundering, anyway?" I asked. "You always hear about it on the news, but I have no idea what it is."

"Me neither," she said. "But I don't think they actually wash the money in a washing machine. So that's not it."

We sat and thought.

6

"We should talk to them," I said. "Maybe we can find out more."

"Are you crazy?" she asked. "What are you going to do, just go up to the house and ask them?"

"No," I said. "We need some excuse to go there. Like, we're selling something. Then maybe we can peek into their house. Maybe we'll see a clue."

"We could buy a pizza and deliver it," Annie said. "Except, if they didn't order it, that would seem strange."

"We could say it was a mistake. Wrong address."

"OK, let's try it."

I rode my bike into town and used some of my fixing-things money to buy a pizza, then rode as fast as I could back to our house, hoping the pizza would still be warm. It is not easy to ride a bike and hold a pizza at the same time. I dropped it a couple of times. I hoped they wouldn't notice.

Annie was waiting at the lab.

We walked down the road to their house. It was a big house, a mansion, with a long driveway winding through the woods. Way out at the end of their driveway, they had already put out their garbage cans for pickup tomorrow. One had fallen and rolled into the road. I picked it up and moved it off the road so no cars would hit it.

We walked down their long driveway, shaded by the woods. When we got to the yard, we saw lots of statues and fountains. The fountains were all dry. At the house, all the shades were still down.

We rang the doorbell. It echoed in the house. A long series of chimes, like church bells.

We heard footsteps. Heavy footsteps.

The red-haired guy opened the door. He was just as grungy as the guy I had seen in the hardware store. He didn't look like he had spent two afternoons doing laundry. He was wearing old sweatpants with ink stains on the sides. It looked like he had gotten his hands dirty and wiped them on his pants. A hundred times.

I tried to peek around him, into the house, but he only opened the door a crack.

"Yeah?" He looked at me. He looked at Annie. He looked at the box of pizza.

"Pizza delivery," I said, holding it out. "That will be $10.50."

He opened the door a little wider. Behind him, I could see a fancy living room. White rug, gold chairs, yellow curtains. No one in it. Boring. No clues.

"We didn't order any pizza," he said. "What is this?"

The blond guy showed up behind him and shoved him aside. "Who ordered pizza?"

"You did," I said. "I'm from Ralpha's Pizza, and you called in for a delivery."

"No, we didn't."

"Well, maybe someone made a mistake," I said. "Or it was a joke. Sometimes people do that, you know. Sorry!" I turned to leave.

"How much is it?" the blond guy asked.

I turned around.

"$10.50," I said.

He took a big wad of bills out of his pocket. It was such a big, thick roll, I couldn't believe it even fit in his pocket.

Suddenly I realized I didn't have any change. I hadn't thought he would actually buy the pizza! I felt Annie thinking the same thing.

I put my hand in my pocket, to stall for time. I pretended I was looking for change. "Uh, I don't think I have change...."

He peeled a $20 off his roll of money and handed it to me.

"Keep the change," he said. "I don't care who ordered it. I'm hungry."

"Thanks!" I said.

He shut the door.

We ran down the driveway and back down the road to my house.

Darius Quinton Coleman, Boy Genius

7

"Let's put this money in our crime-fighting fund," I said, when we got back to the lab.

"We don't have a crime-fighting fund," Annie said.

"We do now," I said. "If we need to spend any more money to figure out what they're up to, we'll use this."

I put the money in an old brass box that my great-grandfather won as a prize in an airshow. It was engraved:

DARIUS QUINTON

DARING AIRMAN

HERO OF THE SKIES

We talked for a while, then Annie went home. She had homework. I stayed in my lab. I liked to sit in the lab and think. Just like my great-grandfather.

The way I think is by drawing. I draw everything. When I'm thinking, I get a notebook and a pencil and just draw anything that comes into my mind. My great-grandfather used to do the same thing.

Never erase, he once told me. *If you erase, you might lose an idea. Just move to an empty part of the page and start over. Or use another sheet of paper. But don't erase, and don't throw any of your ideas away. You never know when you might want to go back and look at that old drawing that you thought was a mistake. If you erase it or throw it away, you can't do that.*

Some of his most brilliant ideas were things he thought were wrong at first.

I drew the crooks' house, Annie's house, and my house, with hills and woods in between. I drew their long, long driveway. I drew the giant rocks in the woods, the trees, the bushes. I drew their cars. I drew the garbage cans at the end of their driveway.

Garbage. That was it.

I called Annie.

"Meet me at the end of their driveway at 5:30 tomorrow morning," I said.

"What for?"

"We're going to look in their trash. There might be clues in there. And we have to do it before they're up so they don't see us. And before the trash collectors come."

"Gross," she said. "And I hate getting up early."

"Me too, but that's what you have to do if you want to be a detective."

"On TV they always get to stay up late."

"Well, we're not on TV."

"All right. See you at 5:30."

8

The next day, Annie came over to my house before school. The sun was just coming up over Clammers Bay, but there were already boats out there. Little boats, with one man in each of them. Baymen, harvesting clams.

Annie and I headed down the road to check the criminals' garbage. It was a good thing their driveway was so long. They wouldn't see us poking around in their garbage. They were probably still sleeping, anyway.

"Look at this. This is disgusting," Annie said when she lifted the lid of the first can.

I looked inside. There was the box from the pizza we had delivered. Frozen dinner boxes. Chinese food cartons. Takeout from the seafood place. Greasy paper towels. Used tissues. Disgusting was right.

The second can was filled with office trash. Clear plastic bags full of shredded papers--cut into tiny pieces, too small to put together. The light-green color of some of the pieces looked familiar, but I couldn't figure out why. I scooped up a handful of the tiny confetti and put it in my pocket.

There were also a whole bunch of printer cartridges in there.

"Look at all those cartridges," Annie said. "We have those at our house, but we only use one every few months. How come they have so many?"

"That could be a clue!" I said. "They're doing a lot of printing. A lot of laundry, and a lot of printing."

Annie said, "I know money laundering doesn't have anything to do with laundry, but we should look it up, just to find out."

"OK," I said. "I have a computer in my lab."

We went back to the lab, got online, and looked it up. Annie was a speed reader, unlike me. If we had to wait for me to look it up, it would have taken all day.

"This could be a beautiful scientific partnership," I said.

"What are you talking about? " she asked.

"Look at you. You're a speed reader. I'm horrible at reading. If we combine our brains, just think what we could do."

"You're horrible at reading? I thought you were supposed to be a genius."

"I am a genius. But I think in pictures, not words, so reading is hard for me. Everyone has something that's hard for them, no matter how smart they are."

She thought about it. "You're right. What about school? Is it hard for you? All that reading?"

"I don't go to school. My mom homeschools me. She changes the lessons around so there's less reading, and more drawing and doing."

"Wow, that's awesome."

"I think so. It takes less time than regular school, because there's only one student. No waiting around while other kids get yelled at or get things explained to them. No announcements, no waiting for papers to get handed out, switching rooms, stuff like that. So it only takes us a few hours a day."

"What do you do the rest of the time?"

"Work in my lab. Build machines. Fix broken appliances for grownups. Hang out with other homeschooled kids."

"There are others?"

"Lots of them. You just don't know about them if you're in school all day. It's like a secret society."

"Wow," she said. "I had no idea. Maybe I can meet some of them sometime."

"Sure," I said.

She skimmed her eyes down the computer screen. Lightning fast. I was seriously impressed.

9

"OK," she said. "Here it is. Money laundering."

She paused. Then said, "The best I can figure out is, they get money from doing illegal things. Then they open some fake business, and they pretend they made the money at that business. But the money is really stolen, or they get it from other crimes. It has nothing to do with laundry or washing machines."

"So we still don't know why they're doing laundry all day but not washing their clothes," I said.

"Nope. I guess we'll have to keep watching them. I'll come over tomorrow after school."

"OK, see you then."

After she left, I walked around our yard. I liked to walk. Sometimes it gave me ideas. I also liked to look at nature. Especially animals. There was a squirrel who lived in a hollow oak tree right outside my lab. Every morning he came out to eat a bite of peanut butter sandwich that I made him. I had rigged up a pulley system with a little bucket. I put the sandwich bite in the bucket and hoisted it up. He came out of his hollow, ran down the branch, took the piece of sandwich out of the bucket, and ate it.

At 8 o'clock, I went into our house and made another peanut butter sandwich, this time for me, and I added honey from my mother's beehive. I went back outside to eat it. Some of the honey dripped out and fell on the grass. Within minutes, bees were all over that honey. "They can smell it," my mother always said. "If you want bees to come around, spill some honey." I watched them suck up all the honey, until they had it all cleaned up. Then I went back inside and started my school work.

I did all my lessons as fast as I could. My mother was thrilled. She sat near me and gave me help and advice when I needed it. The sooner I finished school, the sooner she could get back to her painting. Right now, she was working on a portrait of a man with his Irish Setter dog. She painted them so their eyes seemed to follow you as you looked at the painting. I could never figure out how she did that.

I ripped through math, science, history, and even reading. I wrote a journal entry about my new partnership with Annie.

After school, my mother went back to her painting studio in a little tower on the north side of the house, and I went back to my lab. I sat in my great-grandfather's chair. It was the same place he used to sit when he dreamed up his inventions. He used to draw them at the same table I used. I picked up his pencil--an old mechanical pencil. I used it to draw all my ideas, just like he did.

And I sat and thought. I looked out the high window at the trees. My friendly squirrel jumped out of his hollow and ran along a branch. He dropped an acorn. It bounced off a big rock and rolled down the hill.

I looked back at my paper. I pressed the button on the mechanical pencil so the lead was nice and sharp.

I started drawing.

10

Follow your intuition, my great-grandfather had always told me. *Your brain knows things that you don't know you know. That's your intuition. Never say "No." Never say "wrong," until you're absolutely sure an idea won't work.*

So I drew, and drew, and drew. I drew the three crooks. I drew washing machines. I drew the three guys wiping their dirty hands on their dirty pants. I drew garbage bags full of shredded papers. I drew piles of printer cartridges.

I drew a clothesline. *Why were they washing things all the time?*

I drew another washing machine. I drew money swirling around in it, even though they weren't really laundering money. That was how my mind worked. I drew any idea that came to my mind. Even if it was wrong, because it would lead to another idea. And another. And one of them might be right.

So for now, I was just doodling. And thinking. I drew my way through my thoughts. Sometimes I drew things that I didn't understand until later. I had learned to just draw, without saying NO or WRONG to anything. Just draw. Just like my great-grandfather.

I looked at my drawing of the clothesline. I didn't know what they were washing. It sure wasn't clothes, because they were so dirty. So, I just drew rectangles hanging from the clothesline.

I reached into my pocket and took out the tiny pieces of paper we had found in their trash. I spread them out on my great-grandfather's big oak table. The same table where he sat and drew his flying machines.

The pieces of paper had tiny writing on them.

I got a magnifying glass and looked at them.

I saw letters and numbers.

I saw curving parallel lines. I saw crisscrossed lines.

I saw an eye.

I saw tiny red and blue threads, like miniature strings, in the paper.

I had seen all these things before.

I looked at my drawing: rectangles hanging out to dry. My intuition was trying to tell me something.

I opened the box that held our new crime-fighting fund. I took out the twenty-dollar bill the guy had given me for the pizza.

I looked at it with the magnifying glass.

I saw letters and numbers.

I saw curving parallel lines.

I saw an eye.

I saw tiny red and blue threads.

Hmm. Rectangles hanging out to dry.

I thought about the trash bag full of printer cartridges.

I remembered seeing the guy buying all those cleaning chemicals.

And I figured it out.

These guys really were washing money in the washing machine. They were using all those cleaning chemicals to wash one-dollar bills and take out the printing, including the number ONE and the picture of George Washington on the bill. They ended up with blank rectangles of paper. Then they printed the number TWENTY and the picture of Andrew Jackson on it instead.

See, the paper that money is made with is special. It's almost more like cloth. You can't buy it in any store. So, crooks clean one-dollar bills to get the right kind of paper. Then, they print higher amounts on them. I had heard about this a couple of years before, on the radio, when the police caught some other people doing it.

The shredded-up pieces in their garbage must be bills that they didn't get just right. Ones that wouldn't pass for the real thing.

I felt the $20 they had given me for the pizza. It felt just like real money. Because it was on real money paper. I held it up to the light. Like a shadow, I could see the word ONE hidden in the paper, like a shadow. But printed on the bill, it said TWENTY DOLLARS, and in each corner: 20.

It was a one dollar bill, turned into a twenty.

11

I couldn't wait to call Annie. It seemed like forever until she finally got home from school.

"They're counterfeiters," I said, as soon as she got on the phone.

"Counterfeiters! How do you know?"

I told her everything.

"So what do we do? Call the police?"

"Don't you want to catch them ourselves? Why should we let the grownups have all the fun?"

"Isn't that dangerous?"

"Maybe. But it's a challenge. And I, Darius Quinton Coleman, love a challenge."

We watched their house every chance we got for the next several days. We spent a lot of time with our periscope behind the giant rock.

They didn't go in.

They didn't go out.

But from where we were hiding, behind the big rock, we could smell one thing: clean laundry.

They were washing, and washing, and washing.

"They must be making a big batch of money," Annie said, sniffing the clean-smelling air.

"Maybe before, they were just testing it out," I said. "That's why there were all those shredded bills in the garbage. Those must have been the practice ones. The ones where they made mistakes. Now that they have it just right, they're making a whole lot of it."

"If that's true," she said, "Then pretty soon they'll print a bunch and then they're going to go out and start spending it. So when they leave their house, they'll have it with them in their car. That's evidence. If we can catch them with it, we can prove they're doing it. We'll be heroes."

"That's a great idea!" I said. "I think you might be a genius too."

"Yeah," she said, "But how are we going to stop three guys in a car? They'll run us over."

"Let's think," I said.

But I couldn't think with a pinecone jabbing me in the rear and ants biting my ankle. I needed to go to my lab. I needed to sit in my thinking spot.

"I'll see you later," I told Annie. "You go home and think, and I'll go to my lab and think. Let's check back later."

"OK."

12

On Friday, I sat at my table. I picked up my old mechanical pencil.

I drew the big rock that Annie and I hid behind. I drew the hill sloping down from it toward the road. I drew the squirrel running down the branch toward my bucket of peanut butter bread. I drew an acorn dropping from the tree. I drew springs and gears and levers. I drew a fan and a balloon. I drew a jar of my mother's honey. I drew the three guys in their car, coming around the curve on the road.

I called Annie as soon as I thought she might be home from school. "I have an idea," I said. "We can trap them before they get to town. But it will take some work. I can use your muscles. Are you in?"

"I'm in," she said. "Let's do it."

She came over right away. When I told her my idea, she said, "Those crooks might notice what we're doing. We need a distraction."

"What kind of distraction?" I asked.

"We'll make them think we're over at my house, playing. But we'll really be here, working on our trap."

"How are we going to make them think we're over at your house?" I asked.

"We're going to play, loudly. Let them see us and hear us in your yard. And we'll record ourselves doing it. Then, when we're over here building our trap for them, we'll leave the recording going, over in your yard. Really loudly, so they'll think we're still there."

"Great idea," I said. We got a recorder and went over to her yard.

"Let's play catch," she said.

She went into her house and got a softball. We stood where the crooks could see and hear us through the trees.

I am not a sporty kind of kid. No, I'm more the geeky, nerdy type. And Annie was sporty. So when she threw the ball, it hurt when it smacked into my hand. She was a powerhouse thrower. I wished I had a glove.

"Do you have to throw it so hard?" I asked.

"We have to make it look realistic."

"It'll be realistic when I go to the hospital with three broken fingers."

"Why only three?"

"I like to be precise."

She threw the next two softer, but then she forgot and threw them hard. They hit my hand like bricks.

It was a sacrifice I would have to make, for the sake of neighborhood decency.

We yelled back and forth like we were having a great time. We made so much noise, it sounded like the Yankees were playing the Red Sox. After an hour I couldn't feel my hand any more, and we figured we had enough on our recorder. We left the recorder in her yard, hooked up to speakers, and sneaked through the woods back to my lab. From my house, I could hear us yelling over there. It sounded very realistic.

For the rest of the afternoon, we worked. We strung up ropes. We made a peanut butter sandwich. We rigged up extension cords and antique fans. We filled a balloon with helium from a tank in my lab. We set up gears and drive belts and pulleys. We got a jar of honey from my mother's kitchen cupboard. We got shovels and dug, and dug, and dug, until our backs were aching and our hands were full of blisters. We sawed halfway through a dead tree down by the road. Annie had a lot of good ideas about how to do things. We used a mix of her ideas, and mine, to make a truly crazy criminal-catching machine. My great-grandfather would have been proud.

13

The next day, Saturday, we got up before dawn. We painted two long, thin pieces of rope dark gray, so they would blend into the road. We tied one of them across the road about a foot off the ground. When the crooks came along in their car, they would hit the rope and pull on it. The end of the was tied to a lever that would start our machine.

We tied another painted rope to the dead tree that we had sawed partly through. We let that rope lie on the road. It was almost invisible. When the time was right, Annie would pull it, and the tree would fall.

When everything was set up, I hid in the woods, on the hill between my house and theirs, and waited. Annie was in the bushes down near the road, dressed in old clothes painted with camouflage colors, holding the end of the second rope. We each had a walkie-talkie.

We waited. And waited. And waited. I whispered into the walkie-talkie, "Maybe they're not coming today."

And they didn't. They stayed inside their house all day. It was probably the most boring day of my entire life. Annie's, too.

The next day, Sunday, we got up early again.

"They better come today," Annie said, "Because I have school tomorrow."

We got into our positions and waited.

At nine o'clock I saw their long black car coming down their curving driveway. I held my breath as they came out of the driveway, turned right, and hit the first tightly stretched rope. "They're coming!" I told Annie on the walkie-talkie."

She hunched down behind the bushes and got ready.

The rope across the road was attached to a lever high up in the hollow tree next to my lab.

The lever pushed an acorn out of a cup.

The acorn dropped into the hollow tree and woke up the sleeping squirrel.

The squirrel jumped up and ran out of his hole onto a branch.

On the end of the branch was a bucket with a peanut butter sandwich in it.

The squirrel took the sandwich out of the bucket, and the bucket fell out of the tree.

It hit a knife, which cut the string on a helium balloon.

The balloon floated up and pulled on a switch that turned on a fan.

The fan blew a beachball, which hit a soccer ball.

The soccer ball rolled downhill, and knocked against a giant boulder.

We had spent a long time digging out the ground on the hill below the boulder, so now it was perfectly balanced on the hillside. The tiniest jolt would move it.

The soccer ball knocked it loose.

The boulder rolled downhill, crashing along, picking up speed, and fell onto the road right in front of their car.

They slammed on the brakes just in time not to hit it.

The road in front of them was completely blocked by our giant rock.

Just as they stopped, Annie yanked on her rope. It pulled down the dead tree we had sawed partly through. The tree fell behind their car, blocking them on the other side. They were stuck. They couldn't go forward. They couldn't go back. They could never get their car out of there.

The three guys jumped out of the car. They saw Annie, pointed at her, and started running after her.

"Run!" I yelled to Annie. But she was already running up the hill. She was the fastest runner I had ever seen. They could never catch her.

I ran into the lab and called 911. "Get here quick," I told the operator. "We caught some counterfeiters, and they're coming after us. Send some of your guys to my lab, and the rest to their house. You'll find all the evidence there." I gave both addresses.

Annie sprinted up the hill. Behind her, I could see the crooks huffing and puffing up the hill. They were so out of shape, they had to stop to catch their breath. Too much junk food and not enough exercise.

She got to the lab, and we slammed the door, locked it, and bolted it.

14

"I already called the cops," I said.

"Good," she said.

I went up to the loft, grabbed my jar of honey and poured it out the window, right in front of the door down below. It made a little golden puddle right in front of the door.

One bee showed up to eat the honey. Then another, and another.

The counterfeiters got to the lab and headed straight toward the door.

"You kids!" the red-haired one yelled. "You'll be sorry!"

They stopped when they saw the honey and the bees right in front of the door.

"I'm afraid of bees!" the blond one said. "What if they sting me?"

More bees came. Within minutes there was a swirling cloud of bees blocking the door.

"They're stinging me!" the dark-haired one yelled.

I looked at Annie. "Did you know that bees don't like stinky people?" I said. "My mother always makes sure she's nice and clean when she takes care of her bees."

Annie laughed.

The counterfeiters ran back down the hill, just as the police arrived at the giant boulder that was blocking the road.

The police jumped out of their car and grabbed the crooks. Another police car came. The officers in that one jumped out and ran past the counterfeiters' car, down the road toward their house.

We watched the action from the loft window in my lab. The cops put the crooks in handcuffs, and got them into the police car.

The bees finished cleaning up the honey and flew back to their hive.

Annie and I scraped the rest of the honey out of the jar and ate peanut-butter-and-honey sandwiches to celebrate.

15

The next day, the newspaper headline said, GENIUS KIDS SOLVE CRIME!

The story told how the police had found two big bags of counterfeit money in the car. They had also searched the criminals' house and found the printer, the chemicals, piles of bleached bills, and the other tools they had used to make the fake money.

"Look, we're both geniuses," Annie said. "Not just you. At least, the paper thinks so."

"I think so too," I said. "I could never have done it without you. You had some great ideas."

She smiled. "It was a lot of fun, wasn't it?"

"It sure was," I said. "Here's to a long and beautiful partnership! I think we're going to have a lot of fun together."

About The Author

Kelly Winters is a part-time writer and a full-time mom. She homeschools her son, who struggles with reading comprehension, so contributing a story to the contest was important to her! She is honored to be a part of any endeavor that helps kids become more interested and able readers.

About The Publisher

Story Shares is a nonprofit focused on supporting the millions of teens and adults who struggle with reading by creating a new shelf in the library specifically for them. The ever-growing collection features content that is compelling and culturally relevant for teens and adults, yet still readable at a range of lower reading levels.

Story Shares generates content by engaging deeply with writers, bringing together a community to create this new kind of book. With more intriguing and approachable stories to choose from, the teens and adults who have fallen behind are improving their skills and beginning to discover the joy of reading. For more information, visit storyshares.org.

Easy to Read. Hard to Put Down.

www.ingramcontent.com/pod-product-compliance
Lightning Source LLC
Chambersburg PA
CBHW072233190626
46809CB00017B/1907